Parents and Caregivers,

Stone Arch Readers are designed to provide enjoyable reading experiences, as well as opportunities to develop vocabulary, literacy skills, and comprehension. Here are a few ways to support your beginning reader:

- Talk with your child about the ideas addressed in the story.

- Discuss each illustration, mentioning the characters, where they are, and what they are doing.

- Read with expression, pointing to each word. You may want to read the whole story through and then revisit parts of the story to ensure that the meanings of words or phrases are understood.

- Talk about why the character did what he or she did and what your child would do in that situation.

- Help your child connect with characters and events in the story.

Remember, reading with your child should be fun, not forced. Each moment spent reading with your child is a priceless investment in his or her literacy life.

Gail Saunders-Smith, Ph.D

STONE ARCH READERS

are published by Stone Arch Books,
A Capstone Imprint
1710 Roe Crest Drive
North Mankato, Minnesota 56003
www.capstonepub.com

Library of Congress Cataloging-in-Publication Data
Crow, Melinda Melton.
  Road race / by Melinda Melton Crow ; illustrated by Ronnie Rooney.
  p. cm. — (Stone Arch readers)
  ISBN 978-1-4342-1623-6 (library binding)
  ISBN 978-1-4342-1754-7 (pbk.)
  [1. Dump trucks—Fiction. 2. Trucks—Fiction.] I. Rooney, Ronnie, ill. II. Title.
PZ7.C88536Ro 2010
[E]—dc22
                                                    2008053408

Summary: Three truck buddies compete in a road race.

Creative Director: Heather Kindseth
Graphic Designer: Hilary Wacholz

Reading Consultants:
Gail Saunders-Smith, Ph.D
Melinda Melton Crow, M.Ed
Laurie K. Holland, Media Specialist

Printed in the United States of America.
649

**The little armadillo is a friend of the truck pals.
Every time you turn the page, look for it.
Can you find the little armadillo?**

ROAD RACE

written by Melinda Melton Crow
illustrated by Ronnie Rooney

STONE ARCH BOOKS
MINNEAPOLIS   SAN DIEGO

This is Green Truck.
This is Blue Truck.
This is Dump Truck.

Blue Truck can go fast.

Look at Blue Truck go!

Green Truck can go fast.

Look at Green Truck go!

Dump Truck can not go fast.

Dump Truck has a lot of rocks.

Dump Truck is slow.

Blue Truck drives down the road.

21

Green Truck drives down the road.

Dump Truck dumps his rocks.

Now Dump Truck can go fast!

Go, Dump Truck, go!

Dump Truck is the winner!

STORY WORDS

truck   rocks   road
dump   slow   winner
fast   drives

Total Word Count: 81

Follow your favorite truck pals as they learn about the open road.